The
Brave
Kitten

The Brave Kitten

by Holly Webb
Illustrated by Sophy Williams

tiger tales

For Helena and her beautiful cat Karmel, whose story I borrowed for this book

tiger tales

5 River Road, Suite 128, Wilton, CT 06897
Published in the United States 2016
Originally published in Great Britain 2014
by Little Tiger Press
Text copyright © 2014 Holly Webb
Illustrations copyright © 2014 Sophy Williams
ISBN-13: 978-1-68010-014-3
ISBN-10: 1-68010-014-9
Printed in China
STP/1800/0074/0815
10 9 8 7 6 5 4 3 2 1

For more insight and activities, visit us at www.tigertalesbooks.com

Chapter One

"We'd better hurry, Helena," Lucy said, glancing at her watch and walking faster. "There's a lot to do this morning, with two dogs coming in to be operated on. I need to get everything ready."

"I'll help," Helena said cheerfully, twirling along the pavement in front of her cousin. Helping out at the animal hospital was her favorite. "I can do the feeding and clean the cages on my own. I know what I'm doing."

Lucy grinned at her. "I know you do. You're like the youngest veterinary nurse in the country, Helena — you've had almost as much practice as me."

"I haven't decided yet what I want to be — whether I should be a nurse, or an actual vet," Helena said seriously. "Being a vet's harder. And I'm not sure about doing operations. I don't really like blood. But maybe I'd get used to it."

"You do," Lucy said. "I didn't like it much when I first started training as a nurse, but now it doesn't bother me at all."

"I suppose that cute, lop-eared rabbit has already gone home?" Helena asked. She'd loved petting the rabbit when she'd gone to see Lucy at the animal hospital after school a couple of days earlier. "He was so friendly and— Lucy, what's that?" Helena stopped dancing along the pavement and peered worriedly at the parked car up ahead of them. There was a little mound of pale, sandy fur tucked just underneath the car.

"Oh, no…," Lucy murmured. "Helena, don't look, okay? Just wait there."

"What is it?" Helena asked. She was suddenly feeling a little bit sick, and her heart was jumping. She didn't want to go closer and see whatever it was. But at the same time she couldn't just stay back. The little heap of fur looked like a cat to her, but cats didn't usually lie sprawled like that, not on a road, anyway. Only if they were somewhere warm and safe. "Is it a cat?" she whispered miserably to Lucy, coming closer. "Has it been run over?"

Lucy glanced back at her, frowning, but she could see that Helena wasn't going to stay out of the way. Her cousin loved cats, even though she didn't have one of her own. "I think so. Don't cry, Helena. It must have been quick."

But Helena wasn't listening. "Lucy, look! He moved! I'm sure he did."

Lucy whipped around. The little cat had been so cold and lifeless that she hadn't thought he could still be alive, but Helena was right. He'd twitched, just a bit. "Oh, wow…," she muttered. "We need to get him to the hospital, now. Molly and Pete should be in soon — he's definitely going to need a vet to look at him."

"How are we going to get him there, though? Won't it hurt him if we pick him up?" Helena crouched down by the car, peering at the little cat. One of his back legs was really swollen and seemed to be at a funny angle, and she could hardly see him breathing at all. But his eyes were open now, just a tiny slit of

9

gold. He was looking at them.

"Yes," Lucy admitted. "And he might not want us to touch him, either. But we need to get him there quickly. He's in shock, and I've got a feeling he's been here for a while — he's so cold." She pulled off her big scarf and gently wrapped it around the cat, scooping him up and trying to support the injured leg as well as she could.

Helena watched, biting her lip. She'd seen cats at the hospital hissing and scratching at Lucy and the vets because they were frightened or hurting. She hoped this cat wasn't going to fight — he didn't look as though he had the strength.

Maybe he was just too weak, or maybe he understood that Lucy and Helena were trying to help, but the cat lay still in Lucy's arms as they hurried down the street. Helena was jogging beside Lucy, carrying her bag and looking up at the cat. His head was drooping over Lucy's arm, and from time to time his mouth opened in a tiny, soundless meow.

"You might be hurting him," Helena told Lucy worriedly.

"I know. But we're almost there. Look, I can see Molly's car. She's here already."

Helena pushed open the animal hospital door and looked around. Molly must be out back somewhere, or upstairs making coffee.

"Helena, you hold him." Lucy carefully passed over the scarf-wrapped bundle. "Take him into the back room. I'll go and find Molly."

Helena stood there helplessly. The cat hardly weighed anything at all, and he wasn't moving. She had an awful feeling he wasn't going to survive — he was too weak. "Just hold on," she whispered, as she carried him to the room where Molly and Pete operated. She wondered if she should put him down on the table, but she didn't want to. The table was cold and hard, and she wanted the cat to know that somebody loved him. "Just hold on, *please*.... We're going to make you better."

The golden cat opened his eyes and gazed up at her. He didn't understand what was going on. Everything seemed to hurt and he was frightened. He still wasn't sure what had happened — there had been bright lights suddenly flashing out of the darkness and so much noise. He didn't remember anything after that, until he had woken up at the side of the road and his legs wouldn't work properly.

He had wanted so much to go home, to curl up in his basket, and hide until he felt better. But he was so dizzy and sick, he wasn't really sure where home was. And it hurt to move. He couldn't walk; one of his back legs wasn't working at all and the other one ached. He could only do a strange sort of hop, dragging his bad leg behind him. He'd managed to get a little way up the road, but then he'd felt so cold and tired, he'd hidden under the parked car. Once he'd lain down, it just seemed too hard to get up again.

Now he could feel the warmth of the girl's arms around him. He liked the softness of her voice, too. She sounded gentle, and he rubbed his head against her arm, just a little, to show her he was grateful. But it hurt too much to do anything more, and his eyes flickered closed again.

"Lucy, he woke up a bit, but now I think he's getting worse!" Helena said anxiously, as Lucy and Molly clattered down the stairs and into the operating room. "He's gone really limp. Please say you can help him, Molly. He's such a sweet cat. He hasn't hissed or scratched or anything."

Molly took the cat and laid him carefully on the table. "Definitely a broken leg," she said. "But it's the shock that's really dangerous at the moment. Let's get him on a drip. That'll get some fluids back into him," she explained, seeing Helena frown. "It's a little bit like you having one of those energy drinks after you've been running."

"Oh." Helena nodded, wishing the cat would open his eyes again. He looked so weak. He hadn't even flinched when Molly had moved him.

"Once he's warmed up we can examine him," Molly explained. "I don't want to bother him with X-rays while he's like this. But we can at least check if he's got a microchip, and if he does, we can call his owner."

Lucy passed her the microchip scanner and Molly held it above the cat's neck — but it didn't beep. It didn't make any sound at all.

"No chip," Molly sighed. "Oh, well. We can put a sign up in the hospital window, I suppose."

"But what if his owners never find out where he is?" Helena asked, her voice shaking a little. Life seemed so hard for the poor cat — run over, and now maybe homeless as well.

"Once they realize he's missing, I'm sure they'll call the local vets," Lucy told her comfortingly. But she glanced at Molly. "Are we going to be okay to operate?" she asked. "I mean, he is very skinny. If he's a stray...."

Molly nodded, frowning. "I know. We could send him over to the animal shelter — they'd treat him. But he's so wobbly already, I don't think it's a good idea to move him."

"Why can't you fix his leg here?" Helena asked. She didn't understand what was going on. Surely they needed to operate on the cat as soon as they could! Helena knew that Molly sometimes worked as a volunteer vet at the animal shelter, which helped pets whose owners had problems paying for expensive vet treatments. But why did the cat have to go there?

Lucy put an arm around Helena's shoulders. "It depends on the X-ray,  but he might need to have the broken leg pinned," she explained. "It's a really expensive operation, and then he's going to need to be taken care of for a while. Plus he'll have to have another operation to take the pins out. If he's a stray, there's no one to pay for all that, or for his medicine."

"And even if he does have an owner, they might not be able to afford the treatment." Molly ran her hand over the cat's caramel-colored ears, looking sad.

"You mean, you might not be able to

do the operation?" Helena whispered. "Even if it would make him better?"

"Of course we want to help him," Molly explained. "He's young enough to recover really well. But…."

"You have to!" Helena's eyes filled with tears as she stroked the cat under the chin. "He's so sweet. He nuzzled me…. He's trusting us to take care of him!"

"I bet the animal shelter would help take care of him while he's getting better," Molly said, eyeing the cat thoughtfully. "They might cover the costs if we have to operate, too." She crouched down to be eye to eye with the caramel cat, and gave a firm little nod. "We have to help him."

Chapter Two

The caramel-colored cat lay in his cage, staring out at the dimly lit room. He didn't understand where he was, or what was happening. He was dazed and he felt sick. And there was still something wrong with his leg. It felt worse, if anything. It was aching and heavy, and he couldn't move it properly. It smelled wrong, too — strange and sharp with chemicals. He hated it. Wearily, he pulled himself up on his front legs so he could look at his back leg. It was that weird white wrapping all over his leg that smelled odd.

He leaned over, wincing as the weight pressed on the broken leg, and pulled with his teeth at the bandage that lined the cast. If he could just get that off, then his leg would be all right again, he was certain....

"I wasn't sure you'd be up yet!" said Lucy, smiling at Helena, who was standing outside her front door with her coat on, looking impatient.

"Mom still has her pajamas on,"

Helena admitted, pointing over her shoulder, and Lucy spotted her aunt waving at her out of the kitchen window. "I know it's early, but I really want to see how the cat is."

"I'm sure he'll be fine," Lucy said. "Molly stayed overnight, remember. One of the vets always does when there's a serious case, and she was worried about him. There's a bed upstairs, and she'll have popped down every couple of hours to check on him. 'Bye, Aunt Claire!" she called to Helena's mom. "I'll drop her off in time for lunch — I'm only going in to help Molly out this morning. I hope she's managed to get some sleep," Lucy added to Helena. "That bed's really lumpy. We'll go and make her a cup of coffee and some toast."

But when they got to the animal hospital, Molly was already up, and she looked upset when she opened the front door for them.

"What's wrong?" Lucy asked.

"I don't know how he did it." Molly shook her head in frustration. "I checked on him a couple of hours ago and he was still dozing. He looked fine. But I've just been in, and he's pulled the cast off." She sighed. "We went with a cast because it was a fairly simple break, but at this rate he's going to make it worse."

"Can you put another cast on?" Helena asked, as they followed Molly inside.

"We'll have to. But the more he messes around with that leg, the longer it's going to take to heal. We'll just have to keep an eye on him. He'll probably need a cone collar on now to keep him from trying to tug the cast off, but he'll hate it, and he's pretty miserable already. This time I'm going to use a special kind of cast that tastes horrible if cats try to chew it, so I'm hoping he'll just leave it alone."

"Poor little cat," Helena said, looking into the small cage where the kitten was stretched out on a blanket. He looked back at her wearily, and she could see how sad he was. He was squashed right into the corner of the cage, as if he was trying to hide from everyone. "I bet he hates being shut up in here."

"He needs to be kept still, though," Lucy explained. "Even if he went home, he'd have to stay in a small room — maybe even a dog crate or something — to keep him from doing something silly."

"Has anyone called about him?" Helena asked Molly hopefully. "His owners?"

Molly shook her head. "No, no one's called. I'd better put up a flyer."

"I could make some on the computer," Helena suggested. "We could print them out and put them up close to where we found him, too. His owners must be really worried about him." She shivered, thinking about how wonderful it would be to have a cat of her very own, and how frightened she'd feel if he simply disappeared.

"Posters would be good." Molly nodded. "Okay. Plaster cast number two...."

"Please don't try and pull this one off," Helena whispered to the cat. He was back in his cage with the new cast on, and she'd brought him some food and water. "And don't put your foot in the water bowl, either. When I broke my arm, I wasn't allowed to get it wet at all."

She crouched down on the floor in front of the cage. There were six of them, in two rows on top of each other, and the caramel cat was in one of the bottom ones. "You look really miserable," Helena told him. "Aren't you going to have any breakfast?" She was whispering, and trying not to stare the cat in the eyes. She knew he wouldn't like it.

Even though Helena didn't have a cat, Grandma had given her a book all about cats last Christmas. It was because Helena had told Grandma her secret Christmas wish, when Grandma had asked what present she might like. What Helena really wanted for Christmas was a cat, but it was a secret because Helena knew that Mom would never let her have one. She'd asked before, lots of times, and Mom had always said no. Helena could sort of see why — her mom was a teacher at the school Helena went to, so they were both out all day. A kitten would be lonely and bored and miserable, and Mom thought it wasn't fair. Helena couldn't help thinking that she could make the rest of the time so special that the kitten wouldn't mind. But she knew Mom wouldn't agree.

Grandma had given Helena a tiny china cat and the book, which had a lot of beautiful photos and all kinds of things one needed to know to be a cat owner. She'd written in the front that Helena might not need it right now, but she would have a cat of her own one day. And meanwhile, please could she come and practice with Grandma's cats, Snow and Smudge, as they were getting big and needed Helena to play with them!

On Saturday Helena had gone home and read everything she could find about cat injuries. After she'd read everything there was in the book from Grandma, she'd gone online to look up more information. Now she was worried that the cat was traumatized by the accident. She'd had to get her mom to explain what traumatized meant. It was that the memory of the accident and the time at the vet's might make the cat really upset, and maybe not very friendly.

That made a lot of sense to Helena.

She'd broken her arm falling off the jungle gym at school and even though that had been a year ago, she'd never gone back on the jungle gym.

Hopefully, if she made the little caramel cat's stay at the vet's as nice as possible, he'd think about that, rather than the car, and the cage, and his leg hurting. *It had to be worth a try*, Helena thought.

The cat sniffed at the food and even though cats didn't really shrug or sigh, Helena was almost sure he did. *I just can't be bothered*, he was thinking — she could tell. He didn't even eat a mouthful.

Slowly, Helena reached into the cage and tickled him under the chin with one finger. He was such a handsome cat, even with the ugly plaster on his leg — a soft peachy color all over, with darker caramel stripes, and no white on him at all, except for his drooping whiskers. His nose was apricot-pink and his eyes were huge and golden. *He is going to be big*, Helena thought, *when he is fully grown*. His paws were enormous, as though he needed to grow into them.

The cat curled himself into her hand a little, enjoying the soft touch of the girl's fingers. He didn't understand why he was here, shut up in this cage. The white thing was back on his leg again and now it smelled even worse, if that was possible. And it had tasted disgusting when he'd tried chewing at it. This whole place smelled wrong. Too clean. He hated it. He wanted to go back to his house and his yard, and his little patch of street. But he didn't know where home was — he hadn't known for a while. He'd gone exploring and then, somehow, he hadn't known how to get back home. He didn't understand it — he had thought he would always know. But it had been a long time now, and he'd been hungry and tired and frightened when he tried to cross that road. Now he was further away from his home than ever.

He almost felt like whipping his head around and nipping at the girl's fingers with his teeth. But not quite. That patch under his chin was his favorite place to be petted, and she wasn't stopping. She'd reached all the itchy parts now, and he wheezed out the faintest breath of a purr.

"Oh! Are you purring?" Helena whispered. "Are you feeling better?" She ran her hand gently over his smooth head, and sighed. "If you don't have an owner, you'll have to go to the animal shelter when you're better, so they can take care of you until someone wants you. I hope you cheer up before then, caramel cat. You're so beautiful, and I think you'd be a wonderful pet. But no one's going to take you home if you just hide at the back of your cage. You'll end up staying at the shelter for a long time."

The little golden cat stayed flopped on his blanket, and Helena tried not to think, *Maybe forever....*

Chapter Three

"So how's the cat now?" Helena's friend Katie asked. "I suppose you haven't seen him since yesterday."

"No, and I bet Mom's going to say it's too late to stop by the animal hospital on the way home," Helena sighed. They were waiting for Helena's mom to come over from the staff room to pick them up from soccer after school.

She usually dropped Katie off at home, too, or sometimes Katie stayed for a snack. "She did let me text Lucy last night, and Lucy said he hadn't taken the cast off again. He still hadn't tried standing up, though, and he'd not eaten much."

"And nobody knows who he belongs to?" Katie asked anxiously. "Poor little cat! What's going to happen to him?"

Helena sighed. "Lucy said that if no one claims him in another day or so, he'll have to go to the shelter. But I don't think anyone's going to want a limpy, miserable cat who won't even come and say hello, even if he is pretty. They're putting a photo of him in the local paper, too. Maybe his owner will see that."

"Sorry I'm late! Are you telling Katie about the cat?" Helena's mom had hurried up behind the girls without them noticing. "I wonder if they've found his owner yet."

"That's just what we were talking about," Helena said, with a tiny sigh. Of course, she did want the cat to go back to his old home. But a little bit of her was imagining him coming home with her instead.

"Don't worry, Helena," her mom said gently. "Even if he has to go to the shelter, it'll be fine. I know quite a few people who've gotten their cats and dogs from there. The animals are taken care of really well, and the staff work hard to find new homes for them."

"I suppose so," Helena murmured.

Katie gave her a sympathetic look — she realized what Helena was wishing. Her family had a big black Labrador named Charlie, and Helena loved to come with her to walk him. Katie knew how much her friend wanted a pet of her own.

Lucy called Helena that evening while she was helping her mom make dinner.

"Has anyone called the hospital

about the cat?" Helena asked her cousin hopefully. "Is he okay?"

"He's eating a bit better, but no, still no sign of an owner." There was a little silence, and then Lucy added, "I told Molly I'd take him home with me in a couple of days. Then I can try to find a home for him when he's better. I haven't broken it to Mom and Dad yet, though."

"Oh, that's great!" Helena squealed, so loudly that her mom nearly dropped a pan of pasta. Lucy lived with her mom and dad, and her younger twin sisters, and their house wasn't far from Helena's. She'd still be able to see the cat all the time. She could go and visit him.

"I wasn't sure the staff at the shelter

would have time to take care of him properly. He needs a lot of TLC, poor thing."

"Definitely," Helena agreed. "Can I stop over with Grandma after my dance class tomorrow? It'll be just as you're cleaning everything up to go home. You know how much Grandma loves cats. I told her about him."

Lucy giggled. "I'm surprised she hasn't been around already. See you tomorrow then!"

"Here he is — he's a bit quiet still." Helena pointed to the caramel-colored cat, huddled in the back of the cage and staring out at Helena's grandma rather grumpily. But he shuffled toward the front of the cage when he saw Helena, and she giggled. "That's right. You'd better be nice — I've brought you a present. Look." She pulled a packet of cat treats out of her pocket and ripped the foil. "Tuna flavor! I think they smell awful, but the websites I looked at said most cats love the fishy ones."

"Beautiful colors in his fur…," Grandma said. "So when are you taking him home, Lucy?"

"Tomorrow, I think." Lucy crouched down to look at the cat with them. "He really needs to get out of that little cage and start exercising his leg a bit more now that it's beginning to heal. He's going to live in the laundry room."

"What did your mom and dad say about it?" Helena asked.

Lucy made a face. "They weren't very happy…. But I explained about the shelter being so busy and I promised we weren't keeping him forever. Mom says I have to do all the laundry if there's going to be a cat living in the laundry room…."

"Are you finishing work now, Lucy?"

Grandma said, looking at her watch. "Do you want a ride home? I haven't seen Emily and Bella for at least a week. We could stop in and say hello."

Emily and Bella were Lucy's little sisters, and Helena's cousins. They were only four. Helena loved going to see them — they were always so funny. Usually when she went over there she was talked into having her hair done in some crazy style, covered in feathers or glitter.

But as she sat in the back of Grandma's car, she couldn't help thinking about the cat — so quiet and sad. How was he going to get along with two crazy four year olds? Not to mention Lucy's dog, Buster. He was about as silly as Emily and Bella, and he chased cats, too.

Helena had seen Lucy hanging onto the end of his leash for dear life when they were out for a walk and a cat strolled by.

Helena hugged Emily and Bella when they jumped on her in the hallway, and let them drag her upstairs and paint her nails bright blue. (Mom would make her take it off again before school, but that was okay.) But she didn't enjoy her visit to her cousins' house as much as she usually did.

She just couldn't imagine that frightened little cat living here, even for a little while. Buster was a terrific dog (Emily and Bella had painted his nails blue, too, and he'd let them), but Helena was sure that if he could smell a cat on the other side of the laundry room door, he wouldn't rest until he'd clawed that door to shreds. It wasn't fair to Buster, either. And the caramel cat would be much too nervous to let Emily and Bella draw pictures all over his cast with sparkly pens.

It wasn't going to work.

"What's wrong, Helena?" Grandma asked as they got back into the car. "You're so quiet."

"The cat...," Helena said worriedly. "I'm not sure he'll be able to cope with

Lucy's house, Grandma. I'm not being mean — it's just that he's still so nervous, and there's so much going on there. I think it'll make him worse."

Grandma sighed. "I was thinking about that, too. But Lucy said he'll be kept in one room...."

"Yeah, but there's no way Emily and Bella will leave him in there," Helena pointed out. "They'll be dressing him in their dolls' clothes the minute Aunt Sam's back is turned."

"Mmmm." Grandma drove down the road, frowning to herself. "I wish I could take him...."

"Snow and Smudge wouldn't like it, though, would they?" Helena sighed. "Everyone already has cats, or dogs, or twins." She was silent for a minute, and then added, "Except us. Me and Mom. Mom's always said no, because it wouldn't be good for a cat to be left alone, but this cat needs to have some peace and quiet. Don't you think so, Grandma?"

"And I could always stop in and see him at lunchtime. Give him some attention." Grandma darted a hopeful glance at Helena. "You know, maybe we could persuade your mom together."

"She already said he was beautiful when Lucy showed her the photo on her phone." Helena wound her hands together, over and over. She was suddenly so excited she couldn't keep still.

They just had to convince her mom....

Chapter Four

"But we can't…. We don't have anywhere to keep him."

"We do, Mom! In here — in the kitchen would be all right. He couldn't jump on the counter. We could put a blanket in that space under the counter for him, with his food bowls and litter box, and I promise I'll clean it out."

"I can come and check on him at lunchtime, Claire," Grandma suggested.

Helena's mom frowned, looking around at her little kitchen.

"He can't go to Lucy's house, Mom," said Helena. "And he'll be miserable at the shelter, I know he will. No one's come to claim him, even though we put posters up all around where we found him, and in the animal hospital window. He's in the paper today, with a message saying to call the hospital, but no one has yet. Maybe his owner will see the photo, but he was so thin, Lucy thinks that could mean he's been a stray for a while. I want to be able to take care of him. It feels like I have to, since I was the one who found him."

Helena's mom was silent for a moment, then she turned around to look at her daughter. "I suppose so. Oh, Helena. It's going to be a lot of work, you know. But I am proud of you."

"You mean … yes?" Helena asked, confused. She'd expected to have to beg for an awful lot longer than that. And even then, deep down, she'd been almost certain that her mom would never agree.

"Yes. I mean, we'll have to give him back if his owner contacts the hospital, but yes. Do you think he could stay there until the weekend?" her mom asked. "Then we'd have two whole days to get him used to being at our house before we have to leave him on his own."

The cat was sitting up the next afternoon when Helena brought her mom to meet him. He peered out of the cage bars, waiting for her. He could hear her talking to someone in the next room, and she sounded excited and happy. She had brought him cat treats the last time she came, fishy ones that he liked. And sometimes she opened the front of the cage and sat for a while, stroking his fur and talking to him. She made him feel safe. Even when he was stuck here in this place that wasn't his home, and he could smell the dogs at the other end of the room.

He sat up, wondering if maybe she'd let him out of the cage this time. He could sit on her, and then she'd be able to pet him better and rub his ears.

When he saw the girl come in, he skittered nervously back, knocking his cast against the floor of the cage. She wasn't alone — the young woman was with her, the one he saw every day, and someone else, too.

"It's all right," Helena said soothingly. "This is my mom. We'll be taking you home to our house soon...."

The caramel cat didn't know what Helena was saying, but he liked hearing her soft voice. And the other person spoke softly, too.

"He's beautiful, Helena. Even more so than in the pictures. What are we going to call him? Or have you named him already?"

Helena opened the door of the cage, and the cat stepped out slowly, sniffing at her outstretched hand. She rubbed the dark caramel stripes between his ears, and smiled at her mom.

"I haven't really named him. But when I think about him, I call him the cat with the caramel fur. Do you think we could call him Caramel?"

"We're here!" Helena said gratefully, turning around to peer at the cat carrier strapped into the back seat. Caramel had been howling dismally ever since Mom drove off. He clearly hated the carrier, and didn't like the feeling of the moving car at all.

"Do you think being in a car reminds him of the accident?" she asked her mom worriedly.

"No. I think all cats hate being in boxes. Shut in them, I mean. They like getting in by themselves." Her mom turned off the engine, and looked around, too. "Even when he's been in the cage at the vet's for an entire week, it's not the same. He can't see out of that carrier very well. He'll be much better when we let him into the kitchen."

"It'll probably feel huge," Helena agreed, opening her door and going to get the cat carrier out of the back. "We're here, Caramel. This is your house now, too. Just your kitchen for the minute, though. But Molly says you'll be able to have the cast off in about three more weeks, since you're still a kitten, and you'll heal quicker than a big cat." She carried the box into the house as she chatted to him, and her mom came in behind her, shutting the door of their little kitchen. There were only the countertops in there, and the oven and the fridge, and Helena was almost sure Caramel wouldn't be able to jump up on those. So it was a safe place to keep him.

"Look," she said gently, unlatching the top of the box and taking it off, so Caramel could decide to come out when he wanted to. "There's a special soft basket for you. And a litter box. And I'll get you some food."

They had gone to the pet store the

night before and got it all – the travel carrier, and the basket with a cushion, and the food and water bowls. It had been so exciting. Helena had looked at cat toys as well, but they hadn't bought any, not right now. They were all designed for chasing and rolling and batting with paws, and Caramel needed to stay quiet and rest. Helena promised herself she'd go back and get him some of those toys once he was better.

Caramel sat pressed against the back of the carrier, looking around suspiciously. He hadn't understood what was happening when they'd lifted him out of the cage and into this horrible little crate. Then he'd thought that maybe they were going home. It had been such a long time since he'd been there.

He hunched his shoulders, ears laid back, and watched Helena and her mom both watching him. But they were quiet and still, and no one was grabbing at him. The fur along his spine flattened down a little and he padded his paws thoughtfully into the blanket. Then he sniffed and shook his ears, standing up a bit lopsided. This wasn't his old house, of course. But it smelled good. Not like the pet hospital, full of sharp, strong smells that hurt his nose. This place smelled like the girl, and food. He lurched out of the basket, his plastered leg tangling in the blanket, and set out to explore.

"I thought he was never going to come out," Helena breathed to her mom, watching Caramel sniff the doors of the cupboards.

"I know. Why don't you put some food out for him?"

Helena stood up. She tried to do it very carefully and slowly, but Caramel still flinched back against the cupboards when he saw her move. It made her want to cry. "It's all right. I was just getting you some breakfast," she told him. "Lucy said she didn't feed you this morning, just in case you were sick in your basket."

She took one of the tins out of the cupboard and pulled up the ring on the lid. Then she laughed as Caramel hurried across the kitchen floor, his plastered leg knocking on the tiles. "You sound like a pirate cat with a wooden leg," she told him as she put the bowl down.

"I'm so glad he's eating," her mom said, leaning against the counter to watch him.

"I know — I was worried he'd be too upset being in a new place," Helena agreed. "But look at him. He's wolfing that down." She stood up, putting an arm around her mom. "Thanks for letting us have him."

"You're not disappointed?" Mom asked. "I mean, it's not like having a normal cat. He's not very friendly. And he can't sleep on your bed or anything like that."

Helena shrugged. "I know. But he will be able to one day. And I know he's not that friendly yet, but think how special it will be when he *is*."

She crouched down again to watch

Caramel licking his food bowl. He'd definitely gotten his appetite back, and he was making sure to get every last morsel of food. He stood up again, rather clumsily, and licked his whiskers.

Chapter Five

Caramel uncurled himself from his basket as he heard footsteps coming toward the kitchen door. The girl. And probably breakfast. He hobbled to the door to meet her, rubbing hopefully around her ankles. She crouched down to pet him — but he noticed she carefully shut the kitchen door first, so he couldn't dart around it. She whispered to him as she scratched the satin-soft puffs of fur at the base of his ears, and he leaned against her lovingly.

Helena had spent a lot of the weekend sitting next to him on the floor, letting him get used to her being around. She'd even done her homework sitting on the kitchen floor. When Caramel had tried to steal her pencil while she was doing long division, it had been one of the best moments of the weekend. It proved he was happy enough to play.

"I wish I didn't have to go to school today...," Helena told him, as she scooped food into his bowl. "Yuck. This smells disgusting, Caramel. I don't know how you can be so excited about it." She giggled, watching him waltz around her feet, waiting for her to put the bowl down. He still didn't like moving his broken leg much, so that leg stayed still, and the rest of him whirled around like a spinning top.

He started to gobble the food before she'd even put the bowl down, stretching up to get his mouth over the edge of the bowl, and batting at it with one golden paw.

"You're definitely getting better," Helena said, watching happily as he gulped the food down. "Are you making up for all those days at the vet's when you didn't eat properly? I do still wonder if you were a stray for a while before the accident. You're so thin.

And I'm sure your owners would have seen our posters if they lived anywhere near. We put them everywhere."

Caramel was just finishing the food when Helena's mom hurried into the kitchen. She was a little late getting breakfast ready, and she was rushing. She banged the door open without thinking and Caramel shot into the corner, trembling and pressing himself against the side of the cupboard.

"Mom! You scared him!" Helena gasped.

"Oh! Sorry, Caramel...." Her mom shut the door gently and crouched down, holding her hand out for the frightened cat to sniff. "I'm really sorry, Helena, I didn't realize the door would frighten him so much. He's been so good this weekend."

"I know…," Helena agreed sadly. "But I suppose he's still upset, deep down. It's going to take a while for him to get over that." She looked at her mom. "He will be happier again one day, won't he?"

"I'm sure he will."

But Helena didn't think her mom was very sure at all.

"Be good, Caramel." Helena ran her hand lovingly down his silky back. "Get lots of sleep. Grandma's going to come and see you at lunch time, and I bet she'll bring you treats."

Caramel stood in the middle of the

kitchen, looking up at her uncertainly. He wasn't sure what was happening. Since he had arrived at Helena's house, early on Saturday morning, Helena had been with him almost all the time. She had even come down in the middle of the night to check on him. But now she had a coat on, and a bag with her. It looked as though she were leaving him behind.

At his old house, his owner had gone to work most days. Caramel had lazed the time away, curled up on the back of the sofa so that he could watch the people passing in the street. And the cars. Caramel laid his ears back with a frightened little hiss.

Most days he'd slipped out his cat flap and patrolled his territory in the yards behind the house. There were several other cats in the street, and he was one of the youngest and newest, so he'd had to be careful to stay out of their way. But he still had plenty to explore. There was a pond a few houses away, and he liked to watch the frogs. And catch them sometimes. He could creep up on them among the plants around the water. But his owner hadn't liked it when Caramel had brought one home. He had taken Caramel's frog outside, and locked the cat flap so that he couldn't slip out and get it again.

But here, there was no window to watch from, and no cat flap to slip through. He was all alone in this little room. It was better than the cage at the animal hospital, of course, but being shut up still made him want to claw at the door and fight his way out. When would Helena and her mother come back? Maybe they weren't coming back at all. His old owner had fussed over him, and fed him, and loved him, but now he was gone. Maybe Helena was gone, too. Caramel stared anxiously at the kitchen door, hoping to hear them coming back. But there wasn't a sound.

Maybe he could go and find them himself....

Caramel hobbled across the tiled floor, sniffing hopefully at the door out to the yard. There was a faint breath of fresh air around the side of the door — just enough to make him desperate to go out. He scratched at the door, but not very hard. He could already see that he wasn't going to be able to get out.

Wearily, he trailed back to his basket. His broken back leg was aching, not used to carrying his weight. Caramel snuggled into the basket, and hoped that Helena hadn't left him forever. He hoped that she would come back soon.

Chapter Six

"So does anyone have any exciting news from the weekend?" Miss Smith looked around at the class as she finished taking attendance.

"Tell her!" Katie whispered, nudging Helena in the ribs with her elbow. "Helena does, Miss Smith!"

Helena turned pink, but she nodded. "I've got a cat."

"Oh, wonderful!" Miss Smith smiled. "Where did you get him from, Helena? Or her?"

"He's a he. And he came from the animal hospital where my cousin Lucy works," Helena explained. "He was hit by a car last weekend."

Everyone in the class sat up and started listening more closely. Until then there'd been a bit of a Monday-ish feeling going on, and most people had been staring vaguely at the whiteboard, or whispering to each other.

"Hit by a car?" one of the boys asked. "What happened? Was he hurt?"

Helena nodded. "He has a broken back leg. But he was lucky. Usually they have to operate on cats and put pins in, but he just has a cast."

"But who does he belong to?" Miss Smith asked, sounding a little confused. "Was he a stray? Has no one claimed him?"

"No. And the animal hospital even put a little article about him in the local paper. That page where the animal shelter usually puts a photo of a cat or dog that needs a home."

"Oh, that's how we got our dog!" Max called out. "We saw him in the paper."

"The article was in on Wednesday. But still no one claimed him. So we figured it was okay to take him home. We think maybe he's been lost for a while, even before he got hit by the car. He's really thin."

"Show them the photo," Katie suggested, and Helena pulled it out of her bag. She'd brought it in to show Katie and a couple of her other friends. It was Caramel curled up asleep in his basket, and you could see his plaster cast. She passed it around, and all the class murmured about how cute he was and how sad his leg looked.

"He came home with us because otherwise he would have had to go to the animal shelter," Helena went on. "He's been really lucky. All his vet care has been paid for by donations from the shelter he almost went to. Vet bills can be really, really expensive. Hundreds of dollars, my cousin told me."

Helena frowned thoughtfully. Ever since Molly, the vet, had told her that the shelter was helping to pay for Caramel's treatment, she'd been wishing she could do something to help. Something more than just giving them her pocket money. She'd already decided to get her mom to buy their Christmas cards from the shelter — they made very cute ones with cats and dogs in the snow — but it would be good to think of a way to raise some money, too. So that if another cat got hurt like Caramel, it could be taken care of.

Lucy had said that when she'd called the shelter to tell them that they wouldn't have to take Caramel after all, the girl on the phone had been relieved. She'd said they were full. They needed a lot of money just to feed all the animals, let alone pay for vet care.

"Miss Smith, do you think we could try to raise some money for the shelter? Maybe we could have a bake sale or something," Helena asked hopefully. "Mr. Brown said he wanted all the classes to think about fundraising for charities. It was in assembly, back at the beginning of the school year."

"He did...," Miss Smith agreed. "It's a good idea. What about the rest of the class, though? What do you all think?"

"I definitely want to raise some money for the shelter!" Max nodded. "There were so many other dogs there when we went to get Chester. It was really sad — my mom cried."

Everyone in the class was nodding, but Alice, another of Helena's friends, waved her hand at Miss Smith. "Can we do something different, though? Everyone does bake sales."

"That's because everyone likes cake and cookies!" Katie pointed out, and Alice shrugged.

"It's still a little boring."

"So what do you want to do instead?" Miss Smith grinned. "How about a sponsored silence?"

Lots of people groaned, and Helena twisted her fingers in her hair, trying to think. They needed to come up with a good idea and quickly, before people lost interest. Already a couple of the boys were suggesting a sponsored parachute jump. It would just get silly in a minute. She put her hand up, looking hopefully at Miss Smith.

"We should do something that's about pets. Since that's what we're raising money for."

"Like a dog show!" Alice suggested, but Miss Smith shook her head.

"I'm sorry, Alice, but, I don't think Mr. Brown would let us have a dog show in school," she said.

"But we could have a sort of competition," Helena said slowly. "With videos of our pets, instead of bringing the actual pets in! Like a funniest pet competition. We could ask the whole school if they wanted to enter. And the teachers! Mr. Brown has a really cute dog, doesn't he?"

"I could borrow my mom's phone and film Charlie skateboarding," Katie said excitedly. "He's not very good at it, but he loves trying. It's really funny to watch."

"And people could pay a little bit to enter," Helena said, still trying to think it through. "Then we could show all the videos at lunchtime. And sell tickets — oh, and have brownies and cookies for sale, too," she added to Katie.

"I'll ask Mr. Brown about it at lunchtime," Miss Smith said, as the entire class tried to tell her about their pets' funniest tricks at once. "And then maybe we can use computer class this afternoon to make some posters."

Helena hopped impatiently from foot to foot as her mom unlocked the front door. Grandma had sent Mom a text saying that Caramel had been fine at lunchtime. But Helena was desperate to see for herself that he was all right. She rushed in as soon as Mom got the door open, heading for the kitchen.

"Oh! Listen!" she told her mom, stopping in the hall. "He's meowing. And I can hear him — he's gotten out of his basket, and he's coming to see us!" There was definitely a thumping noise coming from behind the kitchen door, as Caramel limped determinedly toward them. Helena giggled. "Maybe I can film you doing your pirate walk for our competition," she told Caramel, as she carefully opened the kitchen door. "Whoa! No running out...." She caught him gently. "Sorry, Caramel-cat. You have to stay in here."

Caramel half climbed into her lap, and rubbed his chin against her school sweater.

"Is he purring?" Mom whispered.

Helena looked up at her and nodded. She actually hadn't dared to say anything. It was only the second time she'd heard him purr. And that first time at the vet's he had only purred for a second or two, very faintly. Now Caramel was definitely purring. A deep, throaty purr that Helena could feel as well as hear.

"He's glad to see us," she whispered to Mom. "He's actually happy!"

Chapter Seven

"He's definitely looking better," Katie said after school the next day, watching Caramel trying to investigate the fridge. Helena had opened it to get out the butter, and Caramel could smell the ham for her packed lunches. It smelled delicious — and very close to his nose.

"He is," Helena agreed happily. "No, you can't climb in there!" She nudged

Caramel back with her toe and closed the door. "Sorry, Caramel."

Caramel stalked away with his tail in the air, as though he wasn't bothered, but his plastered leg made it a little tricky. He was still feeling wobbly.

"He looked sad in that photo you brought in," Katie said. "But now he's cheered up a lot, I think. It's great to finally meet him in person. Caramel! Here, kitty...." Caramel padded cautiously across the floor toward her, sniffing her outstretched fingers, and letting her rub his head and tickle his ears.

"He's much more friendly now," Helena said happily. "I don't think he'd have done that on Saturday when we brought him home. And it's only Wednesday. He's gotten so much better, and in such a short time. When he was still at the vet's, he was so shy and miserable. He's still nervous sometimes, though," she added. "He hates loud noises."

"He walks really well, doesn't he?" Katie said, watching Caramel prowl around their ankles as they measured the ingredients for their cookies.

"He's putting weight on his bad leg a little more now. Before he was sort of hopping, as if he was trying not to put it down onto the ground. He's got another two and a half weeks, and then hopefully he can have the cast taken off. Can you please pass me the sugar?"

The girls were making cat-shaped cookies to sell at the Funniest Pet Show. Mr. Brown, the principal, had said it was a great idea, very creative. He'd told them to go ahead and arrange the show for Friday, when he'd be able to judge.

"Did you send in a video of Caramel with his cast on?" Katie asked. "I filmed Charlie. He was great! The skateboard went out from under his paws and he just sort of stared at it as if he didn't understand what had happened."

"Yes, I sent it, but I don't think he'll win," Helena said, shaking her head. "Some of the others are so funny. Bella's cat trying to drink out of the faucet in the bathroom is the best, I think. It's the way she turns her head upside down, and then shakes all the water off her whiskers. It makes me laugh every time."

Helena and some of the others in her class had been watching all the videos with their teacher during recess and lunch to find the best ones that would be in the show. They'd wanted to put them all in, but there were so many. They had already made more than $80, just from people paying a dollar to send in a video. They also were selling tickets for the show, and everyone in the class was supposed to be bringing some brownies or cookies to sell, too.

"We should have gotten gold

frosting for the eyes on these cookies," Katie said, peering down at Caramel, who'd gone to sit in his basket under the counter, since they clearly weren't going to feed him anything. "I hadn't noticed before what a beautiful color his eyes are."

"I know," Helena agreed proudly. "Mom and I talked about doing the eyes gold when we made the shopping list, but we decided green ones were more common. Caramel's just extra-specially beautiful."

"He looks like he's sulking," Katie said. "Is he okay? He has his nose tucked down inside his basket."

Helena looked down under the counter and sighed. "I think now that he's walking better, it's making him upset being shut in the kitchen. Every time we open the kitchen door, he's there, trying to slip around our legs. He never scratches or bites, but you can tell he's annoyed. His ears go all flat, and his tail twitches. He wants to go and explore."

"Couldn't you let him out?" Katie asked. "Why does he have to stay in the kitchen?"

"Molly — that's the vet — said that if he tried to climb or jump he could jar his broken leg and hurt it again. Even if he were just trying to climb the stairs, he might trip and fall because of the cast. There's nowhere in the kitchen that he can reach to jump up to, but there's enough space for him to exercise his leg muscles. Otherwise his leg's going to be thin and weak inside the cast."

"Oh, I see." Katie nodded. "That makes sense."

"Caramel doesn't think so, though. He thinks we're just being mean." Helena sighed. "Little grumpy-face," she told Caramel lovingly.

Caramel heard her, and looked up. He gazed at her for a moment and then yawned hugely, showing all his teeth and his bright pink tongue.

Helena giggled. "See? That's what he thinks of us."

Caramel sat by the back door, his nose pressed against the narrow crack between the door and the frame. There was something out in the yard, he was sure. He could hear it — a bird, maybe, tapping and twittering around on the little stone patio. He wanted to be out there, too, smelling the smells, chasing the birds. Just feeling the air ruffling up his fur. He hated being an indoor cat.

He paced up and down beside the door for a few moments, letting out a frustrated meow. His leg was so much better now. It felt stronger. He was sure he could even climb a tree, if only they would let him out. Or maybe scramble up onto the top of a fence, just to get a good look around. He wanted to see what the outside was like around here. He was so sick of being stuck indoors.

His ears twitched as he caught a sound from the front of the house — footsteps on the path, and now scratching as someone fiddled with the front door. Helena was back!

No. His shoulders sagged a little. It wasn't the right time. It would be that other lady who comes to check on him.

"Hello, Caramel...." Grandma was squeezing carefully around the door, making sure not to let him get out. "How are you, sweetie? Want a treat?" She brought a packet out of her purse, and Caramel sniffed as she pulled it open. The delicious smell wafted around. But somehow, it just wasn't very exciting. Not nearly as good as the fresh-air smell through the back door. It was starting to rain now. He could smell the wet pavement smell, and hear the heavy, fat drops pattering down on the stone. He wanted to be out in it. Not for long — just enough to feel the freshness, and then dash back in and lick off all the water. It would be so good....

"Oh, it's raining! And I didn't bring an umbrella." Grandma was staring out of the window, looking irritated. "And look, Caramel, they have the laundry outside! Well, that's going to get soaked. And there's Helena's school sweater. I wonder if she needs that for tomorrow.... I'll have to go and bring it all in."

She put down her bag on the counter, and hurried to the door, jingling the keys as she unlocked it.

Caramel hadn't understood what

she was saying about the laundry, of course, but he knew what the sound of the keys meant. She was letting him out! He stood by her feet, his tail twitching excitedly, and his whiskers fanned and bristling. Out! After all this time! As the door opened, he darted around Grandma's feet, his caramel fur brushing against her legs, and hopped down the little step onto the patio.

Grandma was thinking about the laundry, not about Caramel, so she didn't realize what had happened until it was too late. "Oh! Oh, no! You're not supposed to go out! Oh, my goodness...." She left the laundry and went after the cat. "Caramel! Come on ... Caramel ... Kitty, kitty...."

But Caramel
was sniffing at
the flowerpots
and twitching
delightedly at
the feel of the rain
on his fur. He could smell
other cats, which was interesting, and
dangerous, and exciting. And perhaps
a dog, close by, and there was a beetle
walking along in front of his nose.
Everything was good.

"Come here, Caramel, come on,
you'll hurt yourself...." Grandma
reached down and tried to grab him,
but Caramel skittered out of reach, his
cast knocking on the stone paving, and
throwing him off balance.

He hissed as a twinge of pain ran

through his injured leg, and backed away furiously.

"Oh, no…." Grandma hurried after him, but Caramel hissed again, frightened and hurting, and darted away around the corner of the house, up the little side alley where the garbage cans were.

Grandma was chasing him, but he didn't want to be caught. His leg was throbbing as he scurried up the alley, and now there was a gate, shutting him in again. Caramel spat angrily and pressed up against it. He wasn't going to let her grab him! He couldn't be shut up inside again. He thrust a clawed paw at Grandma as she came close and reached to pick him up. Desperate, he squashed himself down and scrambled under the wooden gate, dragging his plastered leg behind him. He struggled, meowing, for a second — and then he was out, at the front of the house, on the road.

Once he'd squeezed under the gate, Caramel hobbled out onto the pavement, going as fast as he could with his plastered leg. He was determined not to let Grandma catch him. He scurried along the pavement and darted behind someone's garbage can when he heard the gate squeak open, and Grandma dash out after him. He could hear her calling, but he stayed tucked behind the can.

Caramel peered out, watching her, and when she hurried off the other way down the road, he pressed himself close against the wall, and slunk away. Everything smelled so good in the damp, rain-fresh air. His leg was aching a little — he hadn't gone so fast or so far on it in a long time — but he didn't mind. He was tired of cages and that tiny room.

The rain had stopped now and the clouds were blowing over. He shivered with pleasure as he felt the warm autumn sun shining down on his fur. That was what he wanted to do! He would find somewhere to lie in the sun. If only Grandma hadn't been chasing him, he could have stayed in the little yard in the back of Helena's house. He was sure there would have been a nice sunny place to curl up. And when Helena came home, she could pet him while he snoozed.

He glanced uncertainly back down the road. He could go and see. He could squeeze back under the gate…. But he could hear Grandma calling him, her voice more and more worried. That high, panicked note made the fur lift a little along his spine, and he hurried on a few steps further.

He couldn't go too far, though, he realized, after he'd gone past a few more houses. It was hard, half hopping along with his cast like this, and he was already getting tired.

He was looking around, wondering where he could go and sleep in the sun for a little while, when he heard it. It drowned out Grandma's shouting — the low rumble of a car, heading down the road toward him.

Caramel's ears went back, and his tail fluffed out to twice its normal size. He had heard cars before, of course. But now the sound reminded him of the accident, and that strange blaze of light, and then waking up to find he couldn't walk.

He whipped his head desperately from side to side as the growl of the car grew louder, and as it roared past he shot into the nearest yard, forgetting how much his leg was hurting, and how tired he was. He had to get away.

Caramel darted under the bushes, not even noticing how wet they were. And then he huddled there, shivering and terrified, and wishing he'd never strayed outside the house.

Chapter Eight

"He got out?" Helena gaped at Grandma as they stood outside the gates after school. She couldn't understand it. For a moment when Grandma had started to explain, Helena had thought that she must be joking — that it was some sort of silly story, but it wasn't.

"I'm so sorry, Helena. I wasn't thinking. It was the laundry, you see — I had to bring it in because of the rain. Oh, I'm not explaining this very well."

Grandma looked exhausted, Helena realized. She'd probably spent a long time trying to get Caramel back in the house. She felt guilty for being angry, but only a little bit. How could Grandma have let him out, when it was so important that he stayed in the kitchen?

"He slipped past me. He was so quick...."

"We might need to get him to the vet's to see if he's hurt his leg." Helena started off down the road toward home, weaving around everyone pouring out of the school gates. Usually they went back to Grandma's house on the days that Mom was working late, but Helena was sure Grandma would understand that she wanted to check on Caramel first.

"How did you get him back in?" she asked, turning to look at Grandma, who was hurrying after her.

Grandma stopped and simply stared at her, and Helena's stomach seemed to lurch inside her. All at once, she knew what Grandma had been trying to make her understand.

She hadn't gotten him back inside. Caramel was lost!

Helena turned back, looking at the road and the cars flashing by, taking everyone home from school. Then she simply ran. She ran all the way home, ignoring Grandma calling after her. After a little while, she couldn't hear Grandma shouting anyway.

Her mouth was dry, her heart racing. She was so horribly certain that as she turned into their street, she would see the little heap of sandy fur again. And that this time, Caramel wouldn't have been so lucky. He had his leg in a cast — how could he get out of the way of a car?

When she turned the corner onto their road, Helena stopped for a moment, panting, her face scarlet. There was no cat in the road, not that she could see. And no crowd of horrified passers-by. She took a deep, shuddering breath and went on, hurrying up their side of the road, and then carefully crossing over and checking the other side, looking under all the cars.

At last she stopped, leaning against the front wall of their house and trying not to cry. Where was he? Grandma had tried to explain that he'd run under the side gate, so he must have come out onto the road. *Maybe he's just hiding somewhere*, Helena thought, with a sudden jolt of hope. She dropped her school bag by the front door, and set off up the road, calling, "Caramel! Caramel!"

But he didn't come, and she couldn't even hear an answering meow. She flinched as a car sped past, wanting to shout after the driver to slow down. What if Caramel ran across the road to get to her?

Would he come anyway? Helena wondered worriedly. Maybe he didn't know her well enough to want to come back. He'd only lived with them for half a week, after all. But he'd been getting so friendly — she had really felt like he was their cat.

Maybe he'd gone back to his old house — his old owner — if he knew where it was. Helena gulped back tears.

"Helena!" Grandma was hurrying down the road toward her. "Oh, I was so worried. You crossed all those roads on your own."

Helena stared back at her. "I'm sorry, Grandma," she said breathlessly. She'd been so frightened, she'd just thought about getting home and finding Caramel, nothing else.

"He's not here, Grandma," Helena said miserably. "I've called and called. Maybe he's gone back to his old home. Or he might just be lost. He might be one of those cats who doesn't have a good sense of direction. He'll never find his way back to us!"

Grandma wrapped her arms around Helena. "We'll find him," she told her. "I'm so sorry, Helena. Surely he can't be far away."

Caramel
could hear
Helena
calling him, and
his ears pricked forward
hopefully. She sounded worried,
but he knew her much better than
Grandma, and he was sure she wasn't
angry. He stirred under the bushes,
trying to gather the energy to get back
onto his aching leg and go to her. But
as he poked his nose out from under the
plants, another car came racing by, and
he pressed himself back into the leaves
with a frightened hiss.

He couldn't move. He just couldn't.
Even though he could hear Helena
calling him again and again, and her
grandma and later her mom, too,

he was too frightened to come out. Every few minutes a car would go by, and Caramel froze, paralyzed by the noise.

He wriggled back even further when a car pulled up outside the house and footsteps echoed beside his hiding place. It was getting dark, and cold. The cold made his injured leg ache even more, and he shivered miserably. The lights came on in the house behind him, and that just made the night seem darker. He wanted to be home, with Helena putting down his food bowl, and watching him eat.

There were fewer cars now, though, he realized. He had been hiding there for hours, waiting for the next one to roar past, his muscles tensed in case it came close. He edged out from the bushes, his whiskers twitching nervously as he sniffed the night air. Helena's house was only a little way down the road. He knew it.

He could get home, if only he were brave enough to come out of his hiding place.

And it *was* home, he realized. He wanted to be back with Helena. Even if they did keep him closed up in that room. The house was safe and warm, and they would take care of him. Caramel limped out of the tiny front yard and crouched by the wall, his ears laid back. No cars. It was time to go.

Helena was sitting curled up in bed, in the dark. She'd tried to sleep — Mom kept coming in and checking on her, and the last time Helena had actually pretended she was asleep. She didn't want Mom to tell her again that it would be all right, and they'd probably find Caramel tomorrow. Mom didn't know that! She was just saying it to make her feel better. And it wasn't working.

Helena sniffed. She had tried so hard to take care of Caramel, but it would have been better if he'd gone to the shelter after all. He wouldn't have been able to run away there, and he'd still be safe. She felt a choking feeling build up in her throat again, and she tried desperately to swallow it back down.

What if they never saw him again?

Helena gulped, and buried her nose in her comforter, trying to muffle the gasping, horrible noises she was making. It was really late — Mom was probably asleep. She sat there, curled up and shaking, tears making a wet patch on her comforter.

He hadn't been hit by another car, Helena tried to tell herself. They had searched all the streets nearby, and they hadn't found him. And Grandma had called Lucy to check that he hadn't been brought into the animal hospital. He was just hiding somewhere. She pressed her face back into the comforter, thinking how cold and frightened Caramel must be. The wind lashed raindrops against her window again — it was such an awful night to be outside.

Then another sound made Helena look up. She could hardly hear it, with the wind blowing, and at first she'd thought it was just the rain. But it wasn't — she knew that noise! That odd knocking, like a pirate walking on his wooden leg. Helena wriggled frantically, trying to unwind herself from her comforter. It was Caramel!

She jumped out of bed, racing to the

window. She could hear him meowing now, too. She threw open her curtains and shoved the window open, leaning down to see into the yard.

And he was there! A small, bedraggled, golden cat, yowling at her in the moonlight. He'd come home!

"Look, Caramel," Helena told him proudly, as she stuck the certificate onto the fridge door with a magnet. "Bella's cat won the prize for the most amazing pet! I told you she would, but you were second! And do you know how much money we raised altogether? Three hundred dollars! That's a lot," she added, as Caramel rubbed himself around her knees. "Yes, I know. You don't care at all. You just want me to get the cat food out. All right."

She looked down at him as she squeezed the food into his bowl. His fur was soft and silky again, and he was only limping a little. Last night, when she'd run downstairs and out into the yard to scoop him up, his coat had been dark and spiky with rain, and he'd looked so miserable. His leg had obviously been hurting, too. She and Mom had dried him with a towel and he'd purred gratefully. Helena had been worried that the rain had softened the cast, or that he'd made the break worse, but Molly had come over and looked at him, and said that luckily it was all right. She thought Caramel was just limping because he'd been putting more weight on his leg than he was used to.

"Only another two weeks," Helena told Caramel as she knelt on the floor, watching him licking the food out of his bowl. "Molly said she was almost sure the cast could come off after that.

Then you'll be able to explore the rest of the house. And go outside."

Caramel sniffed around the edge of the bowl, just in case any food had escaped, and then nosed lovingly at Helena's hand. He yawned and licked his whiskers, then climbed determinedly into her lap. He flopped down, stretching his plastered leg sideways and kneaded at her school skirt with his front paws. He was glad to be home.

Helena giggled, and shifted her feet a little, so she wouldn't get pins and needles. It looked like Caramel was staying for a while.

Leo
All Alone

by HOLLY WEBB

Evie is overjoyed when she is given her very own puppy, Leo. Leo adores Evie — he loves to be cuddled, sleeps on her bed, and welcomes her home from school every day with a wag of his tail.

But it's not long before another new member of the family arrives: Evie's baby brother, Sam. Suddenly, no one has time to take care of Leo, let alone play with him and take him for walks. Soon he finds himself unwanted and all alone....

HOLLY WEBB

Holly Webb started out as a children's book editor, and wrote her first series for the publisher she worked for. She has been writing ever since, with more than 100 books to her name. Holly lives in England with her husband and three young sons. She has three pet cats, who are always nosing around when Holly is trying to type on her laptop.

For more information
about Holly Webb visit:

www.holly-webb.com
www.tigertalesbooks.com

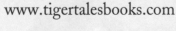